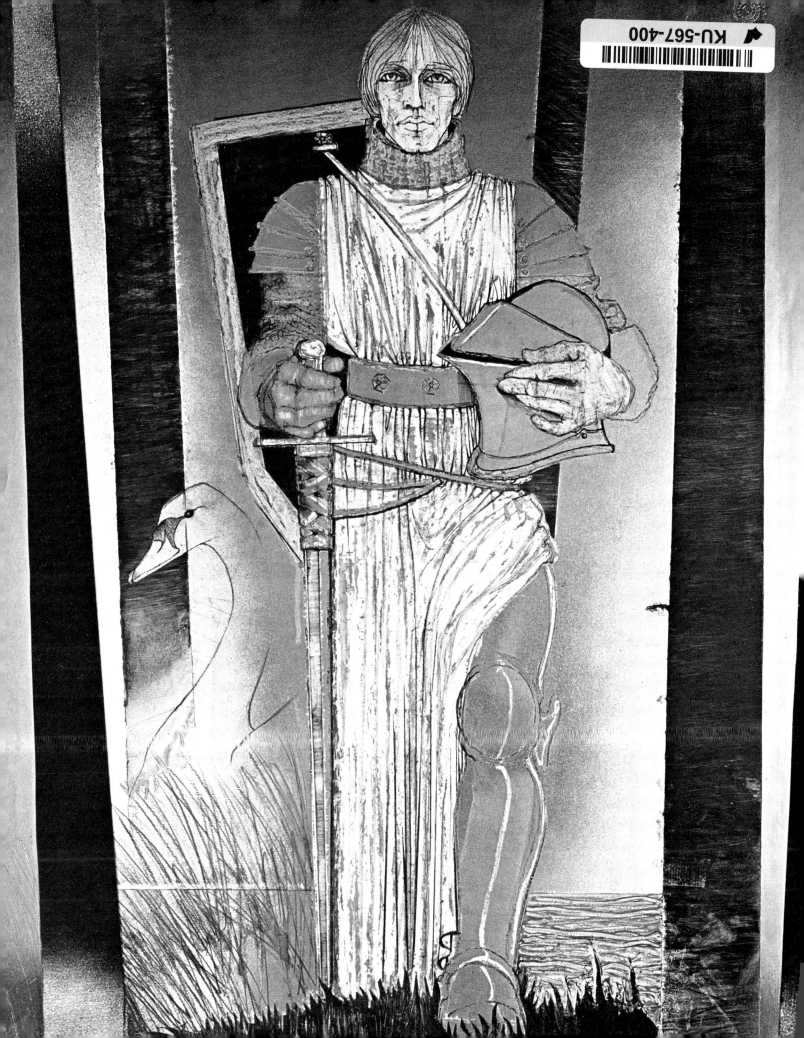

The gentle and beautiful lady who is awaiting the arrival of the knight, a saviour who will rescue her from the false accusations of her former suitor, Frederick von Telramund, is Elsa. The dying Duke of Brabant had entrusted the guardianship of his kingdom, his son Godfrey and his daughter Elsa, to Telramund, a knight and kinsman who wished to make Elsa his bride. But Godfrey has disappeared, and Telramund claims that Elsa has murdered him. He has refused to marry her, and has taken Ortrud as his wife, proclaiming also that, because of Elsa's treachery, he is now the rightful ruler of Brabant.

Elsa is a dreamy girl, who has had a vision. This she describes to the assembled company on the River Scheldt, near Antwerp. She imagines she has seen a knight arrayed in shining armour, sent from heaven to be her champion. He seemed the very incarnation of purity and uprightness. He was leaning on his sword, a golden horn at his side. He had come to give her consolation, and will now be her defender against unjust charges.

"This is the knight I choose; he shall be my champion."...

Telramund's accusations have been made before King Henry the Fowler and his assembled Brabantine people. Henry I of Saxony ruled from 919–936. He was a champion of German rights and German unity. He kept his own house (Saxony) in order while, in foreign affairs, making the whole of Germany safe from invaders. In everything but name he established himself as Emperor of all Germany. In the first scene of the opera we encounter him in Brabant, where he has come to persuade the Brabantines to help him in a forthcoming struggle against perils from the East. On his arrival he is disturbed to find the district riven with feuds. As a wise ruler he is prepared to listen to both Telramund's accusations and Elsa's pleas of innocence. The King is accompanied by a Herald, who plays an important role in the work.

In the German epic *Lohengrin* from which Wagner drew much of his inspiration the dying Duke of Brabant entrusted his daughter Elsa and the guardianship of his kingdom to the ambitious Frederick von Telramund. In the opera Wagner turned Telramund into a dark, lowering figure. He has taken as wife Ortrud, daughter of Radbod, Prince of Friesland. She is more or less a creation of Wagner's imagination. The very opposite of Elsa, Ortrud is the embodiment of evil and deceit and skilled in magic arts, whereas Telramund, though weak, is not wholly bad. Ortrud, unable to love truly, is out to deny Elsa her faith and trust in her supposed saviour. During the first scene she stands by Telramund's side in a cold, haughty attitude, saying little but suggesting by her baleful presence that she is up to no good, for it is really her ambition which drives her husband on, and she is determined that he shall rule in Brabant. It is she who has poisoned his mind against Elsa, and persuaded him to accuse her of Godfrey's murder.

Telramund declares that he is not misled by Elsa's dreamy manner. He says that he has firm grounds for his accusation, and now demands that he should have the chance to defend his honour. Is there anyone who will contest it, he asks? The Brabantines all declare that they are on his side. The King states that God's judgment shall be divined through a mortal combat. Elsa says that she will accept her defender as her husband, and he shall rule over her domain. The Herald, before all the assembled people, calls out for him to appear. Whoever chooses to accept the challenge to fight on behalf of Elsa of Brabant should come forward. Nobody answers, and Elsa's air of serenity changes to one of uneasiness. Telramund taunts her with her inability to produce a champion. Elsa asks the King if he can be summoned again. The Herald repeats his request – again with no success.

Elsa now falls on her knees in fervent prayer, asking that the rescuer that she has dreamt about may be sent to her. Her women support her plea. Suddenly a boat appears on the river; it is drawn by a swan. In the barque is Lohengrin. The people comment eagerly on his handsome appearance, hailing a miracle.

Telramund is speechless, he and Ortrud amazed as much as anyone else.

In tender words Lohengrin bids farewell to the swan, then greets the King and tells him that he has come to stand as champion for a maid slandered by a grievous charge. He turns to Elsa asking if she will entrust her cause to him. She ecstatically accepts his offer. Then we come to the crux of the drama: the shining knight proclaims that if Elsa and her domain are to be his and he is to stay by her side, she must promise him solemnly that she will never ask him whence he came or what is his name. She gravely and readily agrees to this single demand. She and the knight express their feelings in tender words of mutual faith and devotion.

Lohengrin now asks the King to look after her while he turns to Telramund and declares that he has accused Elsa falsely.

Telramund's men urge him not to fight an adversary defended by heaven's might, but he, courageous and proud, says that he will never avoid a challenge. Whatever magic may have brought the stranger there, he does not fear his threats. The Herald now cries out the rules of combat and the King calls on God to grant strength to the arm of the righteous – words that are echoed by the antagonists and their respective ladies in beautifully expressive music.

Six nobles take up position with their lances at their sides while the rest of the knights distribute themselves around the six. The trumpeters sound the call to combat. The King pulls his sword from the ground and strikes his shield with it three times. At the first stroke the combatants take their positions; at the second they draw their swords; at the third they set to. After several violent passages of arms Lohengrin fells his opponent with a tremendous blow. Telramund attempts to resume the contest but staggers, then falls. Telramund's life is forfeit to Lohengrin, but the holy knight generously gives up that right and urges his adversary to repent.

Elsa and all the company rejoice; the hero has triumphed. Only Ortrud stands back, wondering how her plans and hopes for her husband can be salvaged.

As Act 2 begins Telramund and Ortrud are discovered on the steps of the cathedral where Elsa and Lohengrin are to be married. Offstage festive music is heard. Telramund accuses Ortrud of being the cause of his lost honour. He has been banished and shunned because he believed her false story and accused the innocent Elsa. Ortrud rebuffs his verbal attacks, throwing in his face a cry of "Coward!" because a stronger man would have found Lohengrin weaker than a child. She scorns the knight's holy protection, and then proceeds to give her husband new heart. He moves closer to Ortrud as if drawn to her by some sinister force. She tells him that if Lohengrin were forced to disclose his name his powers would vanish – and the only person who can wrest the secret from him is Elsa, whose suspicions of her saviour must somehow be aroused. If that fails Telramund must attempt to lop off part of Lohengrin's body: then his magic spell will likewise be broken. So says Ortrud – and just once more Telramund believes her. Together they swear vengeance.

Elsa appears on her balcony in a white robe and sings of her happiness to the evening breezes. Ortrud approaches her and, feigning meekness and misery, tells Elsa that Telramund is full of remorse for his false accusation. The trustful and innocent Elsa has pity on Ortrud, and opens the door to her enemy. Alone for a moment, Ortrud calls on the gods for vengeance.

When Elsa appears she forgives Ortrud and invites her to join in the wedding procession to the cathedral. Seizing her chance, Ortrud pours doubt into Elsa's ears. Isn't it possible, she says, that this mysterious knight who has arrived as if by magic may just as easily depart in a similar fashion? For the moment, Elsa pities Ortrud for not having her perfect faith.

The day of the wedding dawns. Lohengrin is treated as the country's saviour by the soldiers, nobles and people. The Herald pronounces banishment on Telramund and claims Lohengrin as protector of Brabant. The procession assembles and moves towards the cathedral. Elsa approaches. Just as she sets foot on the cathedral steps Ortrud comes forward. She declares that she seeks revenge for her suffering. Elsa stands back in amazement at this change in Ortrud's behaviour, and asks how the wife of a condemned man can be so arrogant? Pressing her case, Ortrud now says that she at least knows the identity of her husband. Can Elsa name hers? What is his claim to honour and fame? Elsa replies that he is pure and true. Anyone who doubts his mission is condemned to ill-fortune. Ortrud continues to pour scorn on him and to accuse the hero of witchcraft.

At this point the King and Lohengrin, accompanied by their retinue, appear. Lohengrin wonders why Ortrud is by Elsa's side; his bride gives her explanation and asks for protection from the woman. Lohengrin commands Ortrud to stand back, but now Telramund accuses Lohengrin of sorcery and demands to know his lineage. Lohengrin denies Telramund's charge and says his deeds speak for him. But the poison of doubt has entered Elsa's soul, even as she goes into the cathedral to solemnise her marriage to her unknown champion.

The orchestra depicts the bustle and brilliance of the wedding feast. Afterwards, Elsa and Lohengrin retire to the bridal chamber. Each is accompanied by a retinue of, respectively, ladies and nobles. When the two cortèges reach the centre of the room the King presents Elsa to Lohengrin. The pair embrace while the chorus sing a song of celebration and congratulation. Soon the King and attendants leave. Alone, the couple sing of their love and united bliss. Lohengrin says that he was enchanted by her from the moment he set eyes on her. She replies that she had already seen him in her dreams, so that his appearance as her saviour has only made her dream a reality. But the doubts sown by Ortrud soon begin to cloud her happiness. Her name is so sweet in his mouth; maybe one day she will be able to murmur his. She says that perhaps he will be threatened if his name becomes known; if she were able to share it, no power on earth would draw it from her.

As she becomes more pressing in her requests for him to reveal his identity he can speak to her only of his great joy in possessing her, but his attempts to calm her troubled heart are doomed to fail. Becoming more excited and distrustful, Elsa doubts whether he will really remain long with her. She seeks the help of magical powers to bind him to her. At the height of her disturbed and ceaseless questioning Telramund breaks in with four henchmen, swords at the ready.

Uttering a fearful cry, Elsa hands Lohengrin his sword. With a single stroke he kills Telramund. Elsa sinks unconscious to the ground. The terrified nobles let fall their weapons. Lohengrin declares sadly that all their happiness is at an end. Elsa's curiosity has betrayed their love. He orders the body to be carried to the King's judgment-seat. Before it he will reveal his lineage to the assembled company.

After Henry has greeted all his forces Telramund's bier is brought before him. Then Elsa, looking pale and troubled, enters, followed by Lohengrin, who uncovers Telramund's body. He asks if he has done right to strike the intruder dead. He also tells them that Elsa has betrayed him by asking for his name. Now they must all hear his story, and his claim to nobility.

In a distant land, he recounts, there is a castle called Monsalvat. Within it stands a gleaming temple so adorned that it is unlike anything else on earth. Its holiest treasure is a cup blessed with miraculous powers, brought there by an angelic host. Each year a dove descends from heaven to renew its wondrous strength. It is called the Grail, and it gives to its votaries a mystic faith. Those who serve it are endowed with supernatural powers against which evil struggles in vain. Even one sent abroad as a champion of virtue does not lose his holy strength – as long as he remains unknown. If he is recognised he must at once leave.

Now Lohengrin will answer Elsa's forbidden question: he has been sent by the Grail; his father is Parsifal, whose knight he is, and Lohengrin is his name.

The King and the people are overwhelmed with wonder. Elsa's world seems to fall apart as Lohengrin complains bitterly to her that his whole heart and soul had been devoted to her, but that now they must part forever. She implores him to remain; she is full of remorse and awaits her punishment. All her pleas for mercy, for forgiveness, are in vain. Even the King's wish cannot prevent Lohengrin's departure, although he promises a great victory over the Eastern hordes. When his swan arrives, he bids them all a tender farewell. He tells them that in a year Godfrey, who has in fact been transformed into this very swan, might have returned to life. If he now does so, Lohengrin will be far away. As he says his last goodbye he hands his horn, sword and ring to Elsa.

Ortrud, in triumph, says that she knew all along that this swan, enchanted by her, was Godfrey. Had Lohengrin stayed longer, Godfrey would have been freed. She remains in an attitude of solemn ecstasy but, at his moment of leaving, Lohengrin prays silently: the white dove of the Grail descends and hovers over the boat. Perceiving it, Lohengrin unfastens the swan's chains, whereupon it dives into the water, to be replaced by a handsome youth clad in silver. It is Godfrey, who is proclaimed by Lohengrin as Brabant's leader.

As Lohengrin departs, Ortrud sinks down with a shriek. Elsa greets Godfrey, but after a brief transport of joy she falls lifeless to the ground, in her brother's arms.